in the same series

Sam Pig and his Fiddle
The Christmas Box
Sam Pig and the Hurdy-Gurdy Man

The Adventures of Sam Pig

Magic Water

Alison Uttley

Illustrated by Graham Percy

faber and faber

LONDON · BOSTON

First published in 1939
by Faber and Faber Limited
3 Queen Square London WC1N 3AU
This edition first published in 1988

Printed in Great Britain by
W. S. Cowell Ltd Ipswich

British Library Cataloguing in Publication Data

Uttley, Alison
Magic water. –
(The Adventures of Sam Pig).
I. Title   II. Percy, Graham
823'.912[J]   PZ7

ISBN 0–571–15163–9

Magic Water

It was raining as if it would never stop, and the drops pattered on the footpath and rolled in silver beads down the window-pane. Sam Pig sat on his three-legged stool staring out at the storm. He pressed his round nose against the glass and flicked his curly tail. He drummed his small hooves on the floor with a rat-tat-tat in time with the beat of the rain. He was the only person who really liked rain, and he listened to the singing noise as the water spurted in the rain barrel and ran down the gutters. Now high, now low it went, like a fiddle played by invisible fingers.

'Crowds of silver rain-drops dancing on their toes,
Leaping in the rain-tub, swinging on the rose,'

he warbled, and the rain hummed and murmured in the garden as the dry earth sucked it in. The drops hung like rainbow buttons from the twigs of the pear tree, and the streams of water were silver threads weaving among the cabbage roses.

'Where does it all come from, Sister Ann?' he asked, and he turned to his sister who was working close by.

Ann Pig glanced up from her complicated knitting. She was making a three-cornered cap out of sheep's wool and blackthorn flowers. Tom had found the fleecy wool clinging to the hedge where the flock of sheep had struggled through and he had collected the soft strands for Ann. Bill had washed them and dyed them blue. Sam had picked the blackthorn flowers, and had made a pair of knitting-needles from sharp blackthorn twigs. Now Ann was knitting a pointed cap which could be worn on Sam's head

or used as a basket for carrying mushrooms and
blackberries.

'Knit one, purl one,' said Ann, frowning, and
she twisted the wool over the thorns and
disentangled a butterfly which settled on her
work. Sam had left the white starry flowers on the
knitting-needles, and although Ann thought they
looked very pretty, it was difficult to knit with
bees and butterflies settling on one's needles.

'Where does the rain come from, Sister Ann?'
repeated Sam Pig.

Ann put down her work and considered.

'From the rain clouds,' said she.

'And how does the rain get into the clouds?' asked Sam.

This puzzled Ann. She shook her head. 'I expect it just runs backwards,' said she, but when Sam opened his mouth to ask when, where and why it ran backwards, she stopped him.

'Be quiet, Sam. How can I make a pointed cap if you talk? Knit one, purl one, insert a blackthorn flower, and knit two together.'

There was silence except for the click of the knitting-needles and the buzz of bees which sucked the honey from the white flowers. Sam peered at the darkening sky, and the drenched earth. He could see Bill working in the garden, carrying a watering-can. Tom had gone fishing round the corner. He was lonely and Ann wouldn't talk. Only the rain murmured on, so Sam chanted to it.

'Rain, Rain, on my window pane,
Won't you come in, O Shining Rain?'

'We don't want the rain indoors, Silly Sam,' cried Ann.

'Will you sew some raindrops on my coat?'
asked Sam, leaping off the stool and coming to
her.

'No. Of course I won't.' Ann laughed good-
humouredly and tweaked Sam's twitching ear.
'No one can sew raindrops.'

'You can, Sister Ann. You can do everything!'
whispered Sam, and he looked at the wonderful
knitting on Ann's lap.

Ann pondered his words. Was it possible? She
wanted some little buttons for Sam's coat, and
although her brothers had brought various kinds
from the woods, nothing was right. She turned
over the assortment in the workbasket. A dozen
acorns, a bunch of rosy berries, a collection of
pebbles, and some beans. Certainly a row of
glistening raindrops would be much nicer.

'And I could drink them if I was thirsty,' added Sam hopefully.

Ann went to the door and caught the raindrops on a leaf. She threaded her needle and tried to sew them, but they ran together as quickly as she slipped her sewing-needle through, and fell in a pool on the Sunday coat.

'It can't be done,' she sighed. 'They would make pretty little buttons, Sam, but I can't sew them.'

Then Badger came in. His thick coat was dark with rain, and his feet made large prints on the floor.

'Sewing raindrops, Ann?' he said, shaking himself and sprinkling Sam in a shower-bath.

'I can't do it, Brock,' sighed Ann.

'No, I don't think it can be done,' said Badger, holding a raindrop in his paw. He looked admiringly at the silvery globules. Then he drew out a hair from his tail and threaded the raindrop on it.

'Look, Ann! Now you can sew them on the coat.'

So Ann stitched the raindrops, and gave the coat to Sam. He danced round the room, and the buttons twinkled like diamonds, shaking and changing colour, but clinging to the threads.

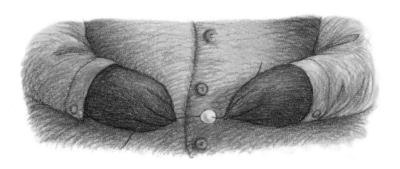

'His buttons were made of raindrops, of raindrops, of raindrops. His buttons were made of
raindrops, and his name was Samuel Pig,' he
sang shrilly.

Bill the gardener came stumping in, with his
wooden spade and his watering-can.

'Whatever are you doing with a watering-can
on a wet day like this?' scoffed Badger.

'Watering the primroses and bluebells,' said Bill, and he swung the can up and down, sprinkling the leafy carpet.

'Can't you see it's raining already?' asked Badger crossly.

'Yes. I'm trying to use it up, Brock. There's such a lot of it all going to waste.'

'He's been filling the watering-can and emptying it all day,' explained Sam eagerly. 'Now he's bringing the rain indoors, where I wanted it.'

Badger grunted, 'Time he had more sense,' and he flung the can in the garden.

Then Tom Pig came in. He carried a fishing-rod and a creel. He wore a green mackintosh and he held a rhubarb leaf over his head for an umbrella. The rain poured off the mackintosh in a pool and Ann ran with a floorcloth to wipe it up.

'It's as wet indoors as out,' she groaned. 'You all come in with your rain and your muddy hooves.'

'Do you want us to leave our feet on the doorstep as if they were galoshes?' asked Bill sullenly. He was upset about the watering-can, for he had been working hard all day.

'Look what I've got,' cried Tom Pig, opening his creel, and the family of pigs crowded round and forgot their irritation when they saw the shoal of little fish lying in the bed of grasses. There were blue fish and red fish and purple fish, all plump and shiny, glimmering like rays of light.

'Caught 'em myself,' boasted Tom. 'Fished 'em up, and caught 'em, and brought 'em home for supper.'

'Where did you get such lovely little fishes?' asked Ann, astonished, and they all exclaimed with delight and held up the slippery morsels.

'You'll never guess! In the rain barrel!' said Tom. 'I've been fishing in the rain barrel all morning. There was nothing at first, and suddenly there was a swarm, like butterflies swimming about, and I netted them.'

'Butterflies don't swim,' grunted Brock. He padded to the door and went outside to the end of the cottage where the rain barrel stood. He peered inside and put in a paw. He brought up half a dozen little coloured fish, green and scarlet and silver, so he dropped them wriggling and squirming back again.

'Never knew such a thing!' he exclaimed. 'Never knew such a lot of fish in our rain barrel! Needn't go to the river now. Fish for breakfast every day.'

'And for dinner and tea and supper,' added Sam, eagerly.

'Fried in fat and stuffed with parsley,' said Bill.

'Roast and boiled and pickled,' said Ann.

Tom put the frying pan on the fire and cooked the supper, and the little fish frizzled and leapt in the pan with the hissing sound of water falling on hot coals. The four pigs and Badger had a merry meal with the piled-up platter of tasty fish.

'Get your fiddle, Sam, and play us a tune, for this rain is beating on the house with a fearful racket,' cried Brock, when he had finished. He leaned back in his armchair and stretched out his short legs. Tom and Bill washed up the supper things, and Ann went on with her knitting. The little fleecy cap was nearly done and very nice it looked with its starry white flowers set among the sheep's wool. Yet something was missing, and she wondered what it was.

Sam reached his fiddle from the hook where it hung from the rafters. He held it under his chin and tuned it. Then he began to play the tunes the rain had taught him. As the music came twinkling and dropping out of the fiddle, Ann knew what

she wanted. She went to the door and into the night. A watery moon was shining and the rain had ceased. Everything was quiet, as if listening to the soft strains of Sam's fiddle. She gathered some more raindrops and then she knitted them into the cap. It was as easy as possible.

When the music stopped, she popped the cap on Sam's head.

'There you are, Brother Samuel. A new cap to wear,' said she.

'It's all sparkling like a waterfall.'

'It's a rainbow in candle-light,' said Badger admiringly.

'It's a dunce's cap,' cried Bill rudely.

'It's a rain cap,' said Sam, and he tossed his head and played another tune.

Now whether it was the effect of the raindrops on Sam's coat and cap, or whether it was the fish

from the rain barrel he had eaten for supper, I cannot tell, but Sam played as he had never played before. His fingers danced over the strings and his little hooves tapped on the floor like a myriad raindrops falling on a wooden roof. He was singing his little song to himself.

'Rain, Rain, Shining Rain,
Come and sing to us, Summer Rain.'

In the midst of the music, as Bill and Tom flicked the drying-cloth about, and Ann beat time with her knitting needles, and Badger waved his pipe, there came a knock, at the door. It was a muffled knock but everyone heard it.

'Only the rising wind,' said little Ann, and she dropped her needles.

'Or the branch of the pear tree tapping,' said Tom, and he broke a cup.

'Or the watering-can fallen against the door,' said Bill, and he knocked over the candle.

'Or a friend come to visit us,' said Badger, frowning at the family of nervous pigs.

'Or the ra-a-a-ain,' whispered Sam, and his fiddle squeaked on the highest C.

The door was slowly pushed open and a

Stranger appeared. He stood in the doorway and
the rain poured from him in dancing cascades to
the floor. He was dressed in black and a long cloak
hung from his shoulders. His hair was shining with
water; the hands which held the great cloak
around him were wet and rain fell from the long
pointed fingertips. His bright eyes were like stars
shining from the darkness. He carried a sheaf of
long arrows, glittering like glass, fine as spun gold,
thousands of them packed into the silver sheaf.

'Let me take your cloak, stranger. You are very

wet,' said Badger, rising, and all the pigs stood waiting near. The Stranger slipped the cloak from his shoulders and held it out with never a word.

It was lined with silver and shining like a fish, wet and glistening with the water which ran down it in streams.

'It's a bad night for you to be out, sir,' continued the Badger.

The Stranger smiled and the rain beat against the house with sudden fury and the wind howled round the house in a hurricane.

He sat down in the chair which Badger offered him and he sipped a glass of wine. Then he stretched out a long arm and took the fiddle which Sam had hung up when the Stranger entered.

'I heard your call,' said he to Sam, and his voice was deep and full of echoes and tremors, so that Sam stared amazed. Across the room hung the silver cloak, and underneath was a pool of water. Little streams rolled down the silken folds and fell on the floor with a patter like a thousand tiny feet. Ann got up and fetched her mop, but the water dripped and ran like a brook under the door and out to the garden. Sighing at the thoughtlessness of strangers, she returned to her seat.

The Stranger was tuning the fiddle with his long slim fingers, and they all waited breathlessly. He drew the bow across and the low wail of a coming storm filled the room. Then he changed his tune, and played airs so entrancing they brought

pictures which seemed to float before their eyes, of rainbow days when light flashes after rain, or spring days when sun and rain strive for mastery. He played like the doves crooning in the woods. 'Coo-roo-roo', their voices came from the fiddle, and the listeners could see the changing colours of

the doves' breasts. He played like the cuckoo
calling in the wet ash trees, and the blackbird
fluting in the pear tree where it has built its nest,
and the thrush singing with beak uplifted to the
rainy sky on the topmost bough of the sycamore
tree.

The water dripped from his black gown, and the

streams ran across the floor, but the family were listening to the nightingale singing to the new moon. They were staring at the Stranger whose bright eyes glittered like the raindrops on Sam's cap, whose face was shadowed and misty as a cloud. He gave the fiddle back to Sam and sat with his legs crossed, his eyes fixed on the fire. But the fire sank low, and the room was filled with damp curling mists and the pigs shivered. They crept silently into their beds and left the Stranger on the hearth.

'Who is he?' asked Sam, but nobody knew. Even Badger shook his head.

'He's very wet, poor fellow,' sighed Ann.

'He never gets any drier,' remarked Bill. 'He will put the fire out and drown us.'

'Maybe he'll go away tomorrow,' said Tom, hopefully.

'I can't send him away,' said Brock. 'There's some magic power in him.'

They came downstairs the next morning and found the floor covered with water. There stood the Stranger, tall and slim, with the raindrops falling from his clothes. He took his cloak from the peg and swung it round his shoulders so that the silver lining flashed and a fine shower of water fell. Then he picked up the sheaf of bright arrows, fine as light rays, and slipped them under his arm.

'Thank you for your hospitality,' said he, bowing low. 'I've not stayed under a roof for many a year, but when I heard that fiddle's music and when I saw that cap of raindrops, I knew I should be welcome.'

'Who are you, sir?' asked Brock, as the Stranger opened the door and stood for a moment on the step. The sun was shining and the world looked beautiful after the storm.

The Stranger didn't speak. Instead he threw back his cloak with a proud gesture, and lifted his long arm with the arrows in his hand, and he seemed to grow in stature to a mighty size. He flung the shining arrows over the earth, and they sped like quivering sheets of rain. He tossed his cloak in the air and it formed a black cloud streaked with silver. He walked swiftly away, and his feet never touched the earth. Birds flew after him, fluttering their wings in the mist of raindrops which encircled him. A rainbow appeared, a great bow across the sky, and the Stranger walked into it and disappeared.

'Who was that?' they asked one another. 'Who was it?'

Brock answered them. 'It was Rain himself,' said he. 'Rain came to visit us.'

They went back to the house, but already the sun was drying the pools of water. The raindrops on Sam's coat rolled away and his cap steamed in the heat. The many-coloured fish swam out of the rain barrel and dissolved in a mist of moonbeams. The flowers raised their heads and tossed the beads of moisture away. The storm was over.

Ann picked up her knitting-needles and the remainder of the fleecy wool. She cast on the stitches and flicked away a bumble bee from the white flowers of her needles.

'I think I will make a sun cap this time,' said she. 'It might keep the poor Rain dry. Do you think he would find it if I hung it in the pear tree, Brock?'

Brock thought that Rain might be glad of it. So Ann knitted another pointed cap and Sam climbed the pear tree and hung it on a high bough. The sun dried it and the moon bleached it, but whether Rain ever took it away I cannot tell you. Certainly the cap disappeared one night in a storm and the next day there was sunshine. Sam thought Rain had worn the cap, and perhaps he was right.